This book is for

_____,

who really should be in bed by now.

For Rowan, with tons of love—LHH

For Tessie, with love from Mom—SH

CLOSE YOUR EYES

A Book of Sleepiness

Lori Haskins Houran

illustrated by
Sydney Hanson

Albert Whitman & Company
Chicago, Illinois

It's bedtime, baby.

I bet you can't wait to

close...

your...

Oh!
You are WIDE awake.

Hmmm.
Let's try something.

A nice bath,

a quiet lullaby,

and a cozy cuddle.

There.
You *must* be tired now.

Or not.

OK. New plan.

Let's NOT go to bed.
Let's stay up!

It will be easy.
We'll ignore anything
soft, snuggly, or sleepy.

Like this baby ape
with a blankie.

And this furry little fox,
all curled up in a ball.

We won't look at those guys.

We won't even *peek*
at this drowsy lamb.

Or these sweet otters,
holding hands
while they snooze.

What's this?
A bunny and a guinea pig,
together?

Come on!
That's not even FAIR!

But it's fine.
Because we're
TOTALLY NOT PEEKING.

Oh no.
No, no, no, no, no.

Say it isn't—

PUPPIES.

Argh!

There's only one way
NOT to see all this sleepiness.

Quick, my love!

Close…

your…

Zzzzzzzzzzzzz.

Also by
Lori Haskins Houran and Sydney Hanson
Next to You
Warts and All

Library of Congress Cataloging-in-Publication
data is on file with the publisher.

Text copyright © 2021 by Lori Haskins Houran
Illustrations copyright © 2021 by Albert Whitman & Company
Illustrated by Sydney Hanson
First published in the United States of America in 2021 by Albert Whitman & Company
ISBN 978-0-8075-1271-5 (hardcover)
ISBN 978-0-8075-1270-8 (ebook)

Printed in China
10 9 8 7 6 5 4 3 2 1 WKT 24 23 22 21 20

For more information about Albert Whitman & Company,
visit our website at www.albertwhitman.com.